To Tucker and Tess, who are fearfully and wonderfully made.

Published by Darling Press LLC
www.darlingpress.com

© 2005 Nancy Tillman

Library of Congress Control Number: 2005901532

ISBN 0-9765761-0-4
10 9 8 7 6 5 4 3 2

Printed in China

On the Night You Were Born

by Nancy Tillman

Darling Press

On the night you were born,
the moon smiled with such wonder
that the stars peeked in to see you
and the night wind whispered,
"Life will never be the same."

Because there had never been anyone like you...
ever in the world.

So enchanted with you were the wind and the rain
that they whispered the sound of your wonderful name.

The sound of your  name is a magical one.
Let's say it out loud before we go on.

It sailed through the farmland
high on the breeze...

Over the ocean...

And through the trees...

Until everyone heard it
and everyone knew
of the one and only ever you.

Not once had there been such eyes,
such a nose,
such silly, wiggly, wonderful toes.

In fact, I think I'll count to three
So you can wiggle your toes for me.

When the polar bears heard,
they danced until dawn.

From far away places,
the geese flew home.

The moon stayed up until
morning next day.

And none of the ladybugs flew away.

So whenever you doubt just how special you are
and you wonder who loves you, how much and how far,
listen for geese honking high in the sky.
(They're singing a song to remember *you* by.)

Or notice the bears asleep at the zoo.
(It's because they've been dancing all night for you!)

Or drift off to sleep to the sound of the wind.
(Listen closely... it's whispering your name again!)

If the moon stays up until morning one day,
or a ladybug lands and decides to stay,
or a little bird sits at your window awhile,
it's because they're all hoping to see you smile...

For never before in story or rhyme
(not even once upon a time)
has the world ever known a you, my friend,
and it never will, not ever again...

Heaven blew every trumpet
and played every horn
on the wonderful, marvelous
night you were born.

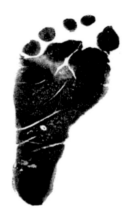

To Nicholas,—"Happy
We wish you, Happy
feet"!! Love,
Jack & Marge
Woods